Looking Good
and Having
a Good Time

Published by Metatron
www.onmetatron.com
305-5555 Ave. de Gaspé, Montreal QC H2T2A3

Copyright © Fawn Parker, 2015
All rights reserved.
ISBN 978-0-9939464-5-5

Editing | Guillaume Morissette
Layout and book design | Ashley Opheim
Cover art | Louise Reimer

First edition
First printing

LOOKING GOOD AND HAVING A GOOD TIME

FAWN PARKER

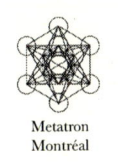

Metatron
Montréal

Vacation with my Mother	7
Doreen, Doreen	17
Kombucha Mother	28
Looking Good and Having a Good Time	49

Vacation with My Mother

***

In July of 2014, I went on vacation with my mother.

We were everywhere together: in the rental house, on the boardwalk, in each other's hair, in the bathroom. I took a bite of a croissant one morning and nipped her thumb.

We stayed in a house by the water with one bedroom and a view of the beach. The floor of our bedroom tilted inward. It tilted further inward every day, I could have sworn. No matter how many times we got up in the night to push our beds apart, they would be touching by morning. God forbid I dropped my hairbrush and it rolled so deep into the floor-crevice that it may as well have been lost at sea.

On the first night, we went walking on Main Street or the equivalent. We passed a big parked truck full of men. They whooped and hollered at us through the windows. They were hoping we were two girls who were looking for a good time and that we were hopefully not mother and daughter, unless we were into that. The man in the driver's seat whistled and my mother said, "Now, now," with her hand. We kept on walking and I swayed my hips a little because I was looking for a good time and I was having one.

In the back seat, like a glimmering star, you caught my eye.

We passed a drunk man wearing a very stylish wig and we laughed until our voices went hoarse. He was sitting on a cloth grocery bag, which he probably could have sold for just under a nickel if it didn't have a man's ass in it.

We walked to a cafe that was open "22 Hours!" It was small inside and we were made to look at each other, eating fat white bagels with jam. A man was playing covers of Johnny Cash songs in the corner, or Johnny Cash was playing his own songs, but I would not have bet money on the latter. The music was making me act very serious, like we were in a weighty movie scene. I wished my mother would play along, but she was talking and talking.

I put too much cream in my coffee and my mouth felt like it was lined with cheap carpeting or like I had taken a mouthful of cheap face powder. Whatever was going on behind my teeth had come at a discounted price for sure.

* * *

In the morning, we went on a boat tour around the shore. I took a photo of my mother on the rail and I got the willies when she smiled for the camera. I had never seen her smile like that, like my camera was a male suitor.

A woman in a big floral dress asked if I would take her photo too. I took one too close and cut off the top of her head, which she could have used to try on different paper hats. I moved back to fit her height into the frame, and there you were again! Your hair and shoulders protruded from behind her head.

You arched your back and dove into the water like the setting sun.

I showed the woman the photos I had taken. In the closeup she looked crazy with her eyes touching the top of the frame and her teeth big and white. In the second one, with you jutting out of her head, she looked like she didn't matter much at all.

"Thank you," she said, and dipped her finger in her cup and sucked the rum off of it.

* * *

Back in the hotel room, I ate expensive mini-bar chips while my mother read a very intrusive celebrity magazine. I felt jealous of how she sat with her painted toenails and her blow-dried hair. I probably could not sit like that.

I finished unpacking my suitcase and sorted its contents on the coffee table: small toothpaste, foldable toothbrush, Burt's Bees Hand Salve, a photo of my parents wearing carved pumpkins on their heads.

I had stolen the photo from my mother's vanity when I went home for Christmas. They were standing outside of their apartment in Toronto in 1986. If you looked closely at the window and squinted a bit, you could see my mother's law textbooks and Thick as a Brick on the record player and my mother buying a lot of cocaine and my father kissing a high school girl.

"What's that?" said my mother, and pointed to the photo.

I crumpled it up and stuffed it into my mouth.

She said, "What's that? What's that?"

I gave her a puffy grin and spit dribbled down my chin.

"Oh, don't," she said.

I went into the bathroom and stuck out my tongue at the mirror.

***

We were on a strip of beach by the rental house when I found a small item that looked alot like you.

"What the heck is that?" my mother said. "It looks like my yoga teacher."

She had it all wrong. She must never have seen her yoga teacher in her life. The contouring and the depth of that ridge with all the dirt and wet sand in it! It looked exactly like you! I put you in the front pocket of my purse.

"Ouch," said my mother. She pulled a small piece of glass out of the bottom of her foot and threw it into the ocean. "Ouch."

***

I was in the kitchen baking banana nut loaf while my

mother soaked her foot in epsom salts. I lined up the ingredients on the counter. Once I got thinking about it, it was hard to ignore the fact that the 4 x 8" loaf pan looked a lot like you. In fact, the three overripe bananas looked like you, and the cup of room temperature butter looked like you, and the beaten egg looked like you, and the teaspoon of vanilla extract looked like you, and the teaspoon of baking soda looked like you and the pinch of salt looked like you, and the handful of chopped walnuts looked like you. You were looking 350° PIPING HOT!

* * *

My mother's foot started to get puffy where she had pricked it with that glass on the beach. I went with her to the clinic in case we found out she was dead. I could barely find a seat in the waiting room with you taking up so much space. I was basically wearing blinders with so much of you in my peripherals.

The doctor came out and said my mother's name. A young boy was spitting teeth into a piggy bank.

I went into the room with my mother while the doctor cleaned her foot with a small white pad.

I asked him if he had any idea why my hair grows so quickly.

He said: "Genetics."

I asked him why I'm afraid of mirrors most of the time.

He said he didn't know.

I asked him why my thoughts race at night, even when I avoid caffeine after 2 p.m.

He said: "Anxiety, probably."

I asked if he had anything that would help me focus long enough to listen to TED talks.

He said: "Yes, probably."

I asked why I spent so much time humming and smiling at strangers and sighing.

He said: "You're in love, I'd say."

Love! Why didn't I think of that.

My mother said: "Ouch!"

* * *

On the last day of our vacation my mother and I went and sat by the water. We had run out of things to say and I was full to the brim with love, so we mostly sat and picked up objects and put them back down.

"What did you do in 1973," I said.

"I left home," she said.

"1975."

"I married my first husband."

"1962."

"My father brought home a whore."

"1983. Who was the whore."

"A whore. In 1983 I met your father."

"1991."

"My mother died." She pointed at a formation of rocks. "I think that's the Canadian Shield. Down the shore."

"Please," I said.

My mother thought every formation of rocks was the Canadian Shield. She thought our dining room table was the Canadian Shield. She thought her fur coat was the Canadian Shield. Once she passed a reflective store window and upon seeing herself, she exclaimed, "Ah! The Canadian Shield!"

* * *

At the airport, I kept smelling my hands and my luggage to remember being on vacation. My mother went to get her car from underground and I exited the airport wearing Love wrapped around me and belted at the waist (Love was an Urban Outfitters culturally-appropriating kimono). My mother pulled up, crying proud and astonished tears. I sprinkled handfuls of love on the heads of a row of bowing children. An emaciated old man crouched at my feet and I rubbed some love into his temples and on the backs of his hands. I saved a bit of it under my tongue for selfish luck.

A group of radical believers said: "Blasphemy! Witchcraft!"

My mother said: "Oh!" (She was still crying.)

The children said: "Rejoice! Rejoice!"

The old man said: "I am healed!"

A news reporter touched my lips with her microphone.

* * *

My mother dropped me off at my apartment at 10:18 p.m. on Saturday. I turned all of the lights on in my apartment and brought my laptop into the kitchen. I made a pot of President's Choice boxed macaroni and cheese and watched Young Teen First Time Anal Sexy Brunette while I ate.

I uploaded photos from our trip to Flickr and emailed a link to my father and my friend Rose.

Young Teen First Time Anal Sexy Brunette said: "Oh fuck oh my god."

I watered all of the plants in my apartment even

though most of them had wilted while I was gone.

Young Teen First Time Anal Sexy Brunette said: "Oh oh oh oh Oh oh oh oh."

I brought my laptop into my room and got into bed and shopped for books on Amazon. I opened another tab and looked at handmade rings on Etsy for Rose's birthday. I thought of you, very far away, diving into the water.

Young Teen First Time Anal Sexy Brunette said: "Ohhhhhhhhhhhhh."

Doreen, Doreen

***

I live in a house in Beaconsfield that John Travolta bought for his ex-wife. It is so big that I get vertigo when I look up at the high ceilings and once I got lost in the boiler room. I stood for hours like a crazy person, contemplating which direction to go.

There is a pillar in the living room that I sometimes think is his ex-wife, dancing in a gown.

I say: What is your ex-wife doing in the living room.
And he says: No, that is the pillar.

Nightly I think about middle age. I will be overweight, I figure, but I keep it at bay with constant movement. I am afraid of my reflection in the bathroom mirror and some of the objects in the kitchen. I leap from the furniture like a cat in the dark.

When I have to pee I make John Travolta walk me down the hallway. He sits in the bathtub and reads our horoscopes out loud from a cheap magazine or calls big companies and puts their hold music on speaker phone. We walk back to the bedroom holding hands and I feel like I'm going to fall.

I throw up most days and call my mother. She has gotten another degree and another boyfriend. The walls in her office are full so she rolls up the certificates and swats flies with them. She writes grocery lists on torn-off scraps of her law degree. At Christmas she wrapped a box of pens in her B.Sc.

She has seven boyfriends who take her on seven dates a week. She has reviewed every restaurant in Toronto on Yelp. There are seven vases on the mantle for seven bouquets of flowers.

She says: My dream is to dance with the dog on his hind legs, and cackles. I tell her about my back, how it hurts when I lie still and it hurts when I move. She walks me through pilates positions over the phone. I do pelvic tilts on the kitchen floor with crumbs poking into my shoulders while my mother counts out sets of ten. I stop doing them eventually and listen to her voice with my eyes closed.

She says: I have never felt like this. She says this once per year, since my father left.

The first time I saw my father in seven years, he laughed until he cried. There was one other time he did this, when I was fourteen and I wrote a list of every way he had ever wronged my mother. This time he was laughing at my new haircut, I was sure.

We were in a diner at Bayview and Belsize. In the middle of a story about my friend Jeffrey, he got up with his mug and walked out of the restaurant and into the snow.

Now he is remarried and I call him on Sundays and he says, "Doreen, Doreen" to his new wife.

My mother hangs up to get in bed with the dog. She carries him up the stairs at night even though he is bigger than her.

***

John Travolta's friend is eating Ativan out of a prescription bottle on the couch. He offers to sell me a pill for five dollars and says, Do you even party.

I flit around the kitchen in my nightdress, packing dry slabs of ham and burnt potatoes into Tupperware containers. When I turn around, the friend rattles his bottle and grins.

Back home, he says, all of my friends are married to older women. They live in these one-stories, and deal drugs right in the living room with their kids walking around, and their dogs.

I go into the bathroom and hide among my precious things. A thick bar of white soap that smells like sweet milk. Gold bobby pins I've bent into dancing legs. My thighs look like big bowling pins against the toilet seat and it feels important that they would look bad in a photograph like this. I stand and feel them, and feel my stomach.

John Travolta and his friend get into the cupboards and eat all of the chocolate I have been hiding. Lindt bars with almond slivers and a broken cream-filled Santa Claus. I come out of the bathroom and the friend says, Do you have any alcohol. Do you have any more chocolate.

He falls off of the couch and we leave him when we go to bed. He wakes up hourly and moves around in the kitchen. I yell from the bedroom, You threw up on my good shoes you animal.

* * *

Gregory is a German tutor with an interactive website. To get to his "About Me" page I had to drag my cursor through a series of medieval-themed mazes. It took 45 minutes to confirm that I had found the right page. He is a 39-year-old man from Eau Claire, Wisconsin. He likes to fly fish when he isn't home "rocking out" with his kids. He edits poetry for *Rat King Anthology*. We exchanged a series of emails, throughout which he used phrases like "showy" and "no patience."

I walk into the Irish Embassy pub and stand still by the bar. I am wearing a green sweater with embroidered pink and yellow tulips. It's the only thing I brought from Toronto when I moved. A girl I was dating stole it off someone's chair in Salvador Darling, and we ran down the street holding pint glasses under our shirts.

Gregory is at the back of the room in a thick turtleneck and waves me over. He is red and drunk and has already ordered me a rum and coke. He's got a copy of my poem on the table in front of him.

What I like, he says, is what you're trying to do here. We argue over the bar's loud 90s rock and my vision swims. I feel like I'm going to faint, or die, and I tell Gregory again and again that it's not about him. This happens to me, it's fine.

I lie down on the rug and it moves in waves under me.

I say: I just think, um.

Symbols are symbols of nothing, he says, and waves the poem in my face like a fan.

* * *

I'm wearing red sequined polyester. John Travolta brought me into the bar in his coat like a shiny pocket watch. We have been fighting between pints of dark beer, being loud and showy. I turn my chair so I'm facing away from him and he pounds the table with his fist. Talk to me, he says. Talk to me.

I go to the bathroom and he follows me in and looks at me and I turn away. He pins me to the wall and holds my face in one hand.

I'm scared, I say.

He says: I'm scared too. I'm scared of you.

His arms are unmovable beams. I throw a tantrum like a child and hit his chest with my fists.

You do it too, he says again and again.

A woman walks into the bathroom and takes out her makeup piece by piece. I catch her eye and she says, Bonsoir.

I break free and run out of the bathroom and out through the front door of the bar. I call my friend Lorraine and say, I need you, I need you.

John Travolta comes outside with my coat and puts it on me and snatches my phone out of my hand. He gets up close to my face and I tell him, I hate you, I'm gone, like some drunk starlet.

There's a man smoking outside of the bar and I say, Do you speak English, I need you. He says, No, this is none of my business.

* * *

All I know, says Lorraine, is what you sounded like on the phone.

She talks to me like a mother and feeds me bowls of fried rice and sugary cereals. I am on a futon in her living room with my things around me like orbiting moons. I've been sleeping perfectly still and in my clothes. Lorraine is tearing pieces of lettuce into a bowl in her lap. She pulls out the pit of an avocado with her teeth.

There's a Korean drama on TV with the sound off.

John Travolta calls me on my cell phone and I go into Lorraine's room and let it keep ringing, cradled like a small animal in my hands.

* * *

Thursday, 10:41 p.m. My boss forwards me the submissions for *Alien Baby Anthology*. My pile of things is spreading to some of the chairs in the living room. Individual Clif Bars. Emergen-C packets wrapped in a hair elastic. My red sequined dress, inside out over the back of a chair, and all of the clothes I've borrowed. There is a submission titled "Block of Palm."

PALM PALM PALM PALM PALM
PALM PALM PALM PALM PALM
PALM PALM PALM PALM PALM
PALM PALM PALM PALM PALM
PALM PALM PALM PALM PALM
PALM PALM PALM PALM PALM

There is another titled "You:"

I will beat you up.
My daddy will beat you up.
My big friends will beat you up.
You won't understand the language of not getting beat up.
You will beat yourself up.
We will all beat you up at once.
We will pass you around in a circle and take turns beating you up.
We will beat you up in pairs.
We will broadcast you getting beat up on TV.
We will write about you getting beat up and make kids in school memorize our writing.
We will display stained-glass windows depicting you getting beat up in the churches.

The document consists of 22 more pages.

Another submission is titled "Photo of My Ass" and the document is empty.

The last submission is called "Untitled", containing only:

DOREEN,
DOREEN.

* * *

Heather O'Neill is reading at Monument-National. I show up with no clothes on and sit at the bar. A man is on stage holding a wooden moose, saying, It's a give and take.

John Travolta comes over and sits behind me at the bar. He writes on a napkin: I want to fuck you.

I write: How did she used to like it?

He crumples the napkin into my mouth and gags me.

Heather O'Neill walks on stage and reads all of *Lullabies for Little Criminals* and begins *The Girl Who Was Saturday Night*. The room is all over it, clutching copies of her books to their chests.

A girl I met once in Toronto comes in and sits at a

table alone. I don't know her name, but I slept with her friend one night when his band played at Lee's Palace. He couldn't stay hard, so we listened to Dirty Washing Machine and smoked in his single bed.

We walk out around page 109 and stand outside the bar. All up and down the street, smiling people are sitting down to fancy meals in restaurants. I tell John Travolta that I'm moving into Lorraine's spare room, that I'll have my things ready by the next night. He looks stunned and says that's impossible, we're in love, I'm a sex symbol.

I say: Symbols are symbols of nothing.

John Travolta's friend comes barrelling out of Monument-National with a bottle in each hand and his arms raised up over his head. He's shirtless and his hair is loose and greasy, and he's looking kind of like Jesus. He nods at me, and grins. He hits the curb and goes straight down, and the bottles break against the pavement in his hands.

John Travolta and me and a group of smoking girls stand around him like a campfire.

Kombucha Mother

***

Hank is starfishing, *Girls Gone Wild!*-style, in bed. The Tenant goes in to wake him up, navigating the warm body-stench of the room. The smell is emanating, it seems, from the hot hairy bulb of Hank's stomach. The Tenant hovers. Touching is too intimate, and there's something about speaking to the dead asleep that's as unsettling as speaking to the plain dead. He raps *shave-and-a-haircut* on the nightstand and Hank stirs before two bits. Hank grunts and sits up, pressing his eyes hard.

"Eight o'clock!" the Tenant says.

"No one today."

"Mm?"

"Two cancellations. No students today."

He leaves Hank to change out of his sweat-soaked Ibanez ("Anything But Traditional!") T-shirt. The kids are in the kitchen chewing a paste of cereal and milk, open-mouthed and incognizant. Their bowls of grey-brown leftover milk will be poured back into the carton after breakfast, thick and mucousy with sugar.

Marine is making up a big batch of egg salad and holds out a forkful for the Tenant to taste. He neglects to say there's nothing on God's Green Earth he would like less than a forkful of sulphur and mayonnaise at eight in the morning.

Instead, he says, "How was work?"

She hums, sort of, and her face does this thing where all her features move inward. "It gets lonely in there at night. But I had my book."

"Mm. I think we're gonna work on the EP for a bit today, but we'll keep it down while you sleep. No thanks, smells good though, but yeah, we've got like a few new tracks we've been working on, and this girl from *Vice* is set up to review the EP."

Marine looks tired at him.

"She's cool, like, I think she'll be into it. We've been talking and, like, hanging out."

Hank enters the kitchen and looks at the Tenant like, *Yeah!* The Tenant has this "give me something rock'n'roll" haircut that moves around on his head like a wig when he walks.

* * *

It's become a hobby for Hank and the Tenant, taking the kids' toys and cracking them in the basement. They upload these experimental electronic tracks to a SoundCloud account under the name Kombucha Mother. They've been getting some pretty heavy sounds out of a "Sleep Sheep" that makes forest/ocean/whale noises when you punch it in the gut. They get high down there and "make it *whale*" (Hank says this in a way that makes his eyes bulge like he's being exorcised). He calls it the "Lamb of God," and makes the Tenant bow down before it whenever he enters the basement, even if it's just to get to his room, and even if he's accompanied by a lady.

Hank says, "I feel like I'm constantly shitting. Like I get something going for five minutes and next thing I know, I'm in there taking another shit."

Marine clinks a spoon against the edge of the mixing bowl.

The Tenant says, "Yeah. Yeah, I hear you."

"Like, I'm out, I'm in the clear, I'm going on with my day, buying a coffee, checking my spam folder, and then my mind wanders for one minute and bam there it is, I have to shit again. What is it? Coffee? Is it society? GMOs? The media? Am I shitting out the byproduct of the media?"

"Yeah."

* * *

Hank puts on a Vinnie Moore tape for background noise. He gets antsy when he can hear the refrigerator humming through the ceiling. Vinnie is in a white T-shirt in some fuzzy blue dimension, playing arpeggios like his hands are bionic.

Hank says, "Where are we."

"We have the two remixes of *Love Apples*, and *Street Fighter 5000* up on the SoundCloud, but like, not the final cuts. And *Love Apples*. The original one."

"And that's all going on *Devil's Food*."

"Yeah."

"I want a new toy for *Love Apples*." He's bobbing his head to what Vinnie's playing. "Yeah?"

"Man, we have like seventeen versions of that track."

"Hang on." Hank goes upstairs to rustle through some more of the kids' stuff. Vinnie Moore looks shifty-eyed.

He comes down the stairs, glowing like he's pregnant, and hiding a prize behind his back.

"Big guy struck gold!"

He gets down on one knee and presents an iPhone 3 to the Tenant. "Darling will you crack this with me."

"You're gonna crack your phone?"

"Who do I ever call?"

"Dude, it's like, an iPhone."

"There's a home phone. There's Marine's phone. My kids have twelve phones each. Man, this thing could be crazy."

"Okay. Yeah, okay, let's do it. Open it up."

Hank starts digging around the bottom of the phone with a screwdriver. "I mean, this thing plays music and makes calls and does the whole works, right, so what kind of filthy shit could we start blasting out of it."

He lifts off the back and starts poking around at wires. He's got his tools laid out like a dentist's.

"Nothing?"

The Tenant grabs the "Sleep Sheep" and holds it in his lap.

"No luck yet." He gets his face closer to the phone. "Come out, come out, wherever you are."

He connects another part of the circuit and it produces this weird undulating, "Oooooo."

"Wait, do that again."

Hank backs up his face from the phone.

"Press the one that went Ooooo."

He does it again. The iPhone goes, "Ooooo."

"That's spooky," Hank says. "Sounds like a ghost."

The Tenant nods. "The Ghost of Steve Jobs."

Hank says, "Man! The Ghost of Steve Jobs!" He holds out a pair of needlenose pliers to the Tenant. "Connect this here."

"Hey, Ghost of Steve Jobs, what's it like in heaven?"

"Oooooo."

"Sweet, nice. Is it true about all that heart attack stuff in 2008 or was that just a rumour?"

"Oooooo."

"Does Vice Girl want me?"

"Oooooo."

"That was a no," says Hank. "Is the *Devil's Food EP* solid so far, Ghost of Steve Jobs?"

"Oooooo."

"Yeah!" They high-five.

The GOSJ says, "Oooooo."

* * *

The loft windows are fogged over from the heat and the rain. The room is white-walled with funhouse-coloured everything else. The Tenant is on the edge of the bed with one leg bent over the other in a way that cuts off the circulation to everything under his left knee. He realizes something (restricted circulation: how dire? > everything, really, how dire? > even so, who cares?) existentially freeing and presents it in layman terms to Vice Girl, who seems by her breathing pattern to be mostly awake.

Vice Girl is in bed, a size six in blue American Apparel running shorts, white American Apparel tank top, with long, long black hair covering her face and the pillow and all the good parts of her torso. She looks like a crime scene, chewed up with a mouthful of MDMA, pot, Bombay and tonic, and spit into an Ikea Alvine Ljuv comforter.

She lifts her hair-curtain up and over her front and reaches for her iPhone. She says, "Yeah" to the Tenant's newfound existential freedom. Scrolls past an Instagram photo of three girls in front of a bar bathroom mirror. Azealia Banks from 64 rows back. A middle finger obscuring the view of an art history textbook. Some chick's face.

"But it doesn't matter, right," he continues, "Because what are we aiming for ultimately? We're just like, clinging, and whose grip is strong enough to win a tug-of-war with death? Who do you think you are? Who do we all think we are, is what I'm saying."

"Yeah." She's scrolling Twitter. Checks her notifications lest something slips under the radar of her phone's alert system. "I know, and like why aren't we all just having a good time."

The Tenant feels anxiety with regards to not

having woken up in his own bed. He has mixed feelings about the poster of Charles Bukowski and his ass hurts. Once his foot fell asleep so bad that when he tried to stand up he fell over. No one was there but, wow, humiliating.

She's re-reading one of her own articles about cultural appropriation re: native headdresses. "I had this weird dream," she says. She's touching herself, a little, over her shorts.

"Did you not get off last night?"

Her feet are tanned from her Tom's, or at least the one hanging off the bed in his direction is. He envisions her walking around the downtown area in one canvas shoe, as if Tom's promise of "One for One" meant you got one shoe and somebody else got the other.

"So I dreamt I was at the doctor, and she was giving me a mammogram, so I'm in the machine and I'm in there really tight, but the doctor keeps telling me to dance. She's like, keep dancing, don't worry, keep going."

"Woah." The Tenant drops his head. Grunts and massages his scalp.

Vice Girl is going at herself.

"That's like, pathetic fallacy, sort of," he says. "That the rain just got heavier when you picked up speed."

She makes a noise. The Tenant checks the weather on his phone. Closes all running Apps.

Vice Girl makes another noise.

"Did you come?"

"Yeah."

He turns to look at her.

"Yeah." She pulls the comforter up over her breasts. "Still on for Saturday? You're releasing and everything?"

"Yeah. Saturday at midnight. So, Sunday, then? Whatever. Yeah."

"Okay, I need to have my piece up by Tuesday, so."

"Yeah, no, sure."

* * *

The Tenant feels ambiguous discomfort w/r/t being back in the bungalow. There are gummy splatters of milk on the kitchen table and cat hairs on the washcloths. The coffee maker has Marine's Monday morning brew in it (it's Wednesday) and the wet grounds are experiencing a first-snow-of-the-season kind of situation.

The Tenant throws out Monday's coffee grounds. A small voice is talking in the basement. He gets the Tim Horton's Dark Roast Pre-Ground Coffee out of the fridge.

"Well, yeah, I mean, I knew what I was going into, but I guess I just expected more clarity," Marine says in the basement.

The Tenant pours four cups of water into the back of the coffee maker.

"Like, if it's bad, it's bad, and if it's good, it'll feel good, right?"

He dumps three spoonfuls of Tim Horton's Dark Roast Pre-Ground Coffee into a filter and places it in the coffee maker.

"But nothing's like that, I don't think. I just have this urgency. There's this real urgency in me."

The Tenant turns on the coffee maker and waits and listens.

"Like maybe I'm doing something wrong, or not doing enough. That's it, I think. I feel like I'm not doing enough."

The coffee maker beeps. There's a shuffling in the basement, and the Tenant assumes position, further left and mug in hand.

"Hi," Marine appears in the doorway.

"Hey," he says. "You're awake?"

"Yeah, I took the kids to school today," she says, "and then I got doing some stuff around the house."

The basement lights are on from when Marine was

down there. The Tenant has an inkling she's been messing around with some of their equipment. What's been giving her away, really, is the reoccurring light patch on her face, and it wouldn't take a forensic specialist to know that it matches the smears of foundation on the iPhone 3.

Hank has the iPhone hooked up to a handheld Casio tape recorder, and he's wired it to a switch that turns on the GOSJ's "Ooooo." The Tenant gets him going a couple times.

"Just gonna make a few minor tweaks to you, dude." He pries the back off the phone and digs around inside. Links the GOSJ's "Ooooo" circuit to the tape recorder's on/off switch.

* * *

From the top of the basement staircase, only Marine's foot is visible.

"No."

Her foot shakes.

"No, I couldn't." She giggles.

* * *

Vice Girl is eating some weird thing with chia seeds.

She's leaning over the kitchen island with her chest nearly on the counter. The Tenant's peripherals catch this over his laptop screen and he wonders if there's a potential market for something like a cross between a coaster and a bra, but what would be the point.

"I dug the tracks you Facebooked me."

"Check this out." He opens up Computer/Audio/Marine_Clips and turns the laptop to Vice Girl.

"HOME_LIFE.wav."

"Yeah."

"COOKBOOK.wav?"

"Give it a listen."

The file opens in iTunes: "Haha, yes, it was definitely in good fun, a lot of it. You know, real savoury dishes that look like breakfast foods. They're fun! And it's not a new concept, I'm not inventing anything here, I'm just making it practical and easy. Bob Blumer did it on an episode of *The Surreal Gourmet*. He made this great soup that looked like a bowl of Cheerios, for nightshift taxi drivers. Really cool. So I thought I'd take it a step further."

"What is this?" Vice Girl pauses Marine.

"The family I rent from, it's the wife."

"Did she publish a cookbook?"

"No, that's the thing. She just goes on about this stuff. It's like, really cool."

***

PLEASURE.wav
"Hi. I'm alright. No, I'm fine, I'm okay. Yes, he's at work. At the music school. Hm? I don't know, are you telling me the truth? Haha, I don't know if I believe you, you'll have to prove it to me. Yes, well, yes I guess I am. I think I'd like that. Oh, but I don't know. Are you sure? Okay. Yes, okay."

Marine repositions herself in her seat.

***

"Man, I think you're really gonna dig this." The Tenant opens up the Kombucha Mother SoundCloud, where he's uploaded the final cut of the *Devil's Food EP*. The track listing is as follows:

1. Love Apples
2. Street Fighter 5000
3. Devil's Food
4. Love Apples [Extended Version]

Love Apples opens with ten minutes of silence followed by a big "Oooooo" from the GOSJ. Then comes a few moans of unadulterated pleasure from

Marine. The track really picks up when the "Laughing Giraffe" kicks in.

Hank looks phased.

The Tenant bobs his head to the music. His movement slows with the fadeout of the song.

Hank says, "What is that."

"Like, so sweet, right?"

"What was that at the beginning?"

"The Steve Jobs thing? The Marine part?"

"Have you been recording me and my wife?"

"Dude, no. It's like, all her."

"What?" Hank starts the track over. Turns the volume up. "What the fuck is this?"

The Tenant gets back into nodding along to the beat. He shouts over the music, "I guess it makes sense that this is upsetting for you."

Hank hammers the pause button. "Man, what is that?"

"She's down here all the time, like pretty serious with The Ghost of Steve Jobs. But I figured it was like a masturbation thing, right?"

"She jerks off down here?"

"Well, like, phone sex, now that I think about it."

Hank's eyes look crazy. He's really wigging out about the song, which is somewhat of a pro/con situation, the Tenant feels.

***

CHILDHOOD.wav
"I had these fantasies about hurting things. Vaccinating children and like, giving them shots. Mostly holding them down and saying, I have to. I'm sorry, I have to . . ."

***

The bungalow is quiet. "Okay, my room is downstairs." The Tenant passes a sliver of Marine in the living room, between the open basement door and the hallway. She's hunched over and shaking, he thinks, but can't quite tell.

Vice Girl hovers by his shoulder. Maybe sees it too.

"Right down here," he says. "Yeah, so like, if you hate it, I'll pull the plug."

He turns on the basement light. The iPhone 3 is open-faced, wires ripped out, screen shattered.

"Hang on." He rushes to the recording desk. The phone has been meticulously destroyed, every wire has been clipped.

Vice Girl approaches. "Is that your phone?"

"No, it's—" He scans the desk. The "Sleep Sheep"

is sitting untouched beside the computer monitor. Next to it, the circuit bent giraffe. "Here, wait."

He opens the Kombucha Mother SoundCloud.

***

VICE > MUSIC > INTERVIEWS > JUNE 10 2014

JENNY LEUNG TALKS "CIRCUIT-BENDING" WITH KOMBUCHA MOTHER'S EVAN ABRAMS

Toronto "dirty electro-pop" duo Kombucha Mother have been releasing tracks on their SoundCloud since early 2010, yet they've just released their first EP in May. I sat down with Evan Abrams, one nervous half of Kombucha Mother, in his basement-apartment-cum-recording-studio. Hank, Abrams' partner in crime, lives upstairs with his two kids.

The place is filled with broken toys; old rejects of Hank's kids, spilling wires and labelled crudely with masking tape. Evan smokes a bowl while I set up my recorder.

So what's the deal with the toys?

We crack them. You can get a lot of weird stuff out of most noise-making toys, so we started playing around with them and recording anything that seemed like it would be cool in our music.

"Cracking them" is how you get the sounds?

Yeah. Circuit-bending is what people call it, mostly. We mess around with the wires and it distorts whatever sound the thing has been programmed to make. One of my friends in high school had a "Tickle Me Elmo" and we fucked around with the thing when we were bored one day. It wasn't until a few years ago I discovered that this was actually a thing. Like, there were people out there doing the same thing, but in much cooler ways.

And then you started incorporating it into your music?

Yeah, well I moved into this place in my last year of university. I got hooked up with Hank through Craigslist, and we immediately hit it off. He was teaching guitar out of what's now my apartment and he got offered a job at a music school, so like this place was already set up like a studio, pretty much. I got him into bending and I guess making music just seemed like the thing to do.

So *Devil's Food* is your first "real release." How has the shift from individual singles to a full EP been for you guys?

I mean, it feels like it's been a long time coming. This is our second attempt at releasing the *Devil's Food EP,* actually. We had it all set and ready to go and ended up losing everything— final cuts, samples, some of our equipment—the night before we were planning on releasing. It was rough.

But these are essentially the same tracks?

Essentially. They have like, the same names and they're coming from the same place, but we're like, not a big deal, you know? It's not like I can just Google our name and up comes a hundred sites with our tracks streaming. When our stuff disappeared from the SoundCloud page, it literally stopped existing. So I can't say for sure how similar these songs are to the originals, but they feel the same to me... a couple things have changed.

And you added the track, *For Marine*.

...Yeah. Yeah, that's a new one.

Can you talk a bit about the story behind it?

[Evan scratches at his hands. He starts talking about the song, but gets visibly upset and asks me not to print any more of what he says. He later apologized by email for not "keeping it professional" during the interview.]

Looking Good and Having a Good Time

* * *

Four girls were crowded around Linda with a phone receiver pressed to her ear. Their faces were excited and free in ways she had only ever experienced secondhand, and in ways that made her feel a little ill. Every time you recall a memory, you change it a little bit forever, is something Linda's science teacher told her. So were the screeching free girls she was reminded of girls she had ever even met? Were they a point of comparison for the here and now to the extent that Linda was feeling? Were all pretty giddy girls the same girls, and would Linda be recalled by future generations as the same outsider weirdo she is now?

"Dial a number!" said one girl.

"Do it!" said another.

Linda's finger moved slowly over the keypad, like a big steady robot arm in a carnival game. "I'm thinking," she whispered.

The last time they had a sub and ditched Phys. Ed., one girl made a call and the man on the other end made her tell him in detail about the last time she ate a pear—what type it was and how ripe on a ten-point scale. She told him it was organic and he totally lost it.

Linda wrapped the phone cord around her fingers and prayed to Jesus, or anyone else who happened to deal in small miracles, that she wouldn't accidentally dial the pear guy. She decided to play it safe and dialled the first nine digits of her mother's cell number, and then a 7 (luck) instead of a 4.

The girls closed in. "Is it ringing?"

"Yes," said Linda. "Shhh."

A voice on the other end said: Good afternoon, Serendipity. How may I help you?

Linda slammed the phone receiver back into its hook.

"What did you do that for!"

"Sorry," said Linda.

* * *

Linda's mother's friend, Mr. Donahue, came over for dinner that night because it was his birthday. He was loaded, but he didn't have a lot of other friends. Linda worried he was looking too much at the side of her face during dinner, as he was sitting at the end of the table in prime profile-viewing territory. From the front, she felt she looked mostly like any girl, but from the side, she looked like a cartoon pig. When someone looked at her, the front of her face followed them like a security camera.

Linda chewed and her face burned with being looked at. Dinner always tasted weird when guests were over. She couldn't get it out of her head that someone was eating one of Mom's Classics for the first time. How could this taste to a newbie, she thought, how do we come off to people who don't know the whole story. How does dessert taste to someone who has only ever eaten raw meat and bugs. Probably like when Dad quit smoking and got his taste buds back, and said in front of the children that strawberry wafers tasted like an angel's tits.

Mr. Donahue looked at Linda's cartoon pig profile and said, Linda, have you been researching colleges, and Linda said, Not really, no, and let her mother take it away with a list of fabulously reasonable options.

Linda finished her dinner and answered Mr. Donahue's interesting questions and went upstairs to wrap one of her mother's old belts around her bloated stomach and pose like a supermodel. The thing about this guy that was better than being at her dad's house was that she could get up and leave mid-conversation and he would only feel self-conscious, rather than yell at her.

She sat down by the phone in the upstairs hallway and dialled her mother's number, with a 7 at the end instead of a 4.

"Good evening, Serendipity."

Linda hung up. She could hear the adults laughing downstairs at something one of them said. She called the number again. She could hardly believe that the woman would say her line no matter how many times Linda called. She called again.

"Good evening, Serendipity."

"Yes, excuse me," said Linda. "But what is this place?"

"This is a book store," said the woman.

"What kind of books?"

"All sorts of them," she said. "I bet I have one for you. Something special. What is your name?"

"Linda."

"Alright, Linda. Let me put you on hold for just a moment."

Linda held. Some pretty relaxing jazz music played through the phone receiver into her ear.

"Right," said the woman. "Here we are. I found just the one."

"What is it?"

"The title is *Looking Good and Having a Good Time*."

"Wow," said Linda. "That sounds perfect. How much is it?"

"The price is, um. It's seventy-five dollars."

"Oh, yikes," said Linda. "I don't have that kind of cash."

"Yes well it is a pricey book."

"Would you read me a sample?"

"Yes I guess I could do that for you, Linda. Alright, well first, um. Chapter one."

* * *

Linda showed up to school the next morning looking like a dream. She was wearing layers of pink sequins and cream faux fur and pearls draped over her person. She went and sat smack dab in the middle of the front row and lay her long arms across her desk and fanned her long hair over the back of her chair.

Her hands draped off the edge of the desk like bedazzled ornaments. She sat up straight, like the book said. She tilted her nose up, just slightly.

"What happened," said someone in the back row.

"That's rude," someone else said.

It was working already! Linda turned in her seat and flicked her long hair and said, "Oh nothing really."

Linda was preoccupied with her self-image and neglected to hear a word of her teacher's lecture about *A Midsummer Night's Dream*. What was a more pressing issue, was this early autumn reality. Linda was on fire. She clacked her pink pumps down the linoleum hallways. She feigned bodily warmth so she could pile her hair up on top of her head and show off the versatility of her face with different hairstyles.

She held her cheeks between her teeth just right, like in the book, so her cheekbones looked like shallow bowls. It was good to be gorgeous. She waved hello to her teachers in the hall. They were different languages, beautiful and old, but they understood each other. They all had knowledge.

At lunch Linda bought an iced coffee and held it with her hand clawed over the top and smoked a cigarette on the edge of school property. The Girls came over and found her and said, Linda, who ARE you today.

Linda coughed. "Same old me," she said, real cool. It was important not to let them phase you. Sure, they were chill and all, but their idea of a good time was phoning movie theatres and asking if they show porn. Linda was ready for a little R.E.S.P.E.C.T.

The Girls rolled their eyes big time.

* * *

Mr. Donahue came over for dinner again that night. He really didn't seem to care much about his own apartment. He kept insisting on passing Linda more of whatever she was almost finished eating. At one point, he filled up her glass with wine and she managed to get a sip in before her mother said, "Jordan, my daughter is fifteen," and everyone remembered.

"Mr. Donahue, have you ever heard the one about the Masonic cockatoo," said Linda. That was one she had learned from Chapter 3.

He hadn't, but boy was the table in an uproar when she lay that one on them.

Her mother said, "Okay, everybody catch your breath," and she took Mr. Donahue upstairs to tell some jokes of her own.

* * *

Linda called the bookstore again to get some info from Chapter 5. The book was really starting to get personal. Linda reminisced about the days of pearl necklaces and curling with a flat iron. But that was then and this was the big leagues. The woman walked her through an improvisational exercise involving recalling the first time she reached orgasm, and attempting to harness that experience as consistent output in her everyday life. It sounded like a big load of garbage.

The one and only time that out-of-this-world sensation had blessed Linda had been in the midst of a game of house, in which Linda was the husband and one of her mother's dressmaking mannequins was her wife. She had finally succeeded in courting the pretty lady when her mother walked into her bedroom and found her making love to a linen torso.

They had later gone into a fabric store to pick out materials to make a mother-daughter quilt, because it was important to bond and to have material proof of said bonding, and upon coming chest-to-chest with a mannequin her mother exclaimed, "Take her for a spin, Linda!"

Mortified was not a strong enough word.

"I don't know a lot about that," Linda told the woman. "You might find this hard to believe, but I haven't seen a boy's privates ever in my whole life."

* * *

Linda's life seemed near perfect to her, except for the fact that she was always tired and she often woke up with her face in the shape of a silent scream. She went online and she was everywhere. Her photos had five thousand likes each on Facebook. There was an article in *Star Magazine* titled, "Beauty Queen Appears Out of Thin Air! Key Word: Thin! Look At Those Legs!" Linda's Gmail inbox contained 2 GB of unread emails from companies offering her money.

It was 3 p.m. when Linda finally rolled out of her duvet. There were indents in her knuckles from sleeping with her statement rings and her eyes were sticky with mascara. She worried she might be losing her figure, but there was no way to know for sure beyond squeezing various parts of her body. This lifestyle might not be so easy. She could keep it up, she figured, at least until she had a career. By then, she could let it go; button up all the way. Meek is in in your 30s. What about a taupe cardigan doesn't say, I know what I want, and I want it between the hours of 7 a.m. and 11 p.m. But the present was fabulous, and Linda was going to ride that wave carelessly and indefinitely.

There was a loud honk outside on the street. Mr. Donahue pulled up in his expensive car.

Linda yanked open the window and said, "My mom is at work, Mr. Donahue!"

"Get in the car, Linda!" He squinted up into the sunlight.

"What?" she yelled back.

"Hop in!" he said.

***

They pulled up to a fancy downtown restaurant real smooth, all in one go to show off to the other men watching that parallel parking was nothing to worry about. Linda stepped out of the car first and stood glimmering in the yellow of the street lights.

"What are you looking at," she said. "Are you looking at me because I'm pretty."

The valet looked her up and down, and then looked at Mr. Donahue.

Mr. Donahue said, "Um," and cleared a lump in his throat.

There was a long line into the restaurant, but Mr.

Donahue said something to the host and slipped him a five. He gave Linda the signal: two fingers on either side of his head like an alien with peace sign antlers.

"It's her," a voice whispered. "It's the Internet Star."

As Linda approached the podium, somebody put a hand on her shoulder and stopped her.

"Oh!" said Linda.

It was the media.

What's your secret, the media wanted to know. How do you do it.

"Well," said Linda.

You could be the face of anything, they said. Take our money.

Linda's ears perked at the mention of cold hard cash. She spilled the beans on her how-to treasure chest, maybe neglecting to cite her sources. She scrawled her information into the media's little black book and followed Mr. Donahue to the nicest table in the joint.

***

Linda had never been to Mr. Donahue's apartment before, which made him seem a lot younger and a lot less loaded. There was a cut-out section in the wall between the kitchen and the living room, making his apartment look like a fast food restaurant.

He gave her a tour, lasting just over two minutes, with the final destination being his organized and unremarkable bedroom. He started to get squeamish when Linda got too close to his bed. He started to sweat pretty much everywhere. Sometimes you fool yourself, he said. Sometimes little girls act like women.

He was getting really bummed, so he told Linda to go sit in the living room while he had his alone time. She went and crossed her legs over the chaise longue. She didn't mind, because occasionally people would walk by and turn their heads, admiring the way her something or other looked.

When Mr. Donahue was ready, he came out of the bedroom and tried to cast some mind spells on Linda. He told her she had misinterpreted his intentions and that her mother would only be confused if she heard about any of this. He kneeled down in front of the chaise and asked Linda if he could give her a hug.

"No, I don't think so, Mr. Donahue."

"Just a nice one," he said. "A short nice one."

Linda's body felt like it was going to up and run away without her head. "I don't think I'd like one at all."

He moved to put his arms around her and he

smelled like cinnamon and paper money.

"Mr. Donahue, bug off!" She scrambled off of the chaise and made a run for it. He grabbed hold of her arm, but she yanked herself free and ran into the bathroom.

There was a stained towel hanging on the wall with a big hole in it, and tiny spidery hairs in the sink. Linda gagged. "What do I do, what do I do," she thought, hyperventilating a little. Mr. Donahue was banging on the door and shouting, "Linda, please." She dialled Serendipity's number on her iPhone. The woman started in on: "Good evening, Serendipity."

"I know, I know," said Linda. "I'm locked in a bathroom and there's a full grown man outside. I'm pretty sure he'd like to get busy with me. I am NOT having a good time!"

"Oh boy," said the woman. "You certainly don't sound like you are. But I bet you look great!"

"Can you help me? Where were we? Chapter nine? What does chapter nine say about this situation?"

Thank you to Guillaume, Jay and Ashley, David McGimpsey, Elliot Burns, Soili Smith, my parents and my sister.

Some of the work in this collection has appeared elsewhere. "Kombucha Mother" was originally published in Joyland Magazine.

A Little Death Around the Heart
Marie Darsigny

A Work No One Told You About
Olivia Wood

How to Appear Perfectly Indifferent While Crying on the Inside
Jay Winston Ritchie

Human Toilet
Jason Harvey

I Am Here
Ashley Opheim

I Wanted To Be The Knife
Sara Sutterlin

Interviews
Laura Broadbent

Les Oeuvres Selected
Matthew E. Duffy

Limes
Jasper Baydala

Looking Good and Having a Good Time
Fawn Parker

Magnetic Days
Roland Pemberton

Pony Castle
Sofia Banzhaf

Something Happened to Me
Julian Flavin

Tampion
Ali Pinkney

Teen Surf Goth
Oscar d'Artois

The Title Of This Book Is An Inside Joke
Sophia Katz

TO ORDER OUR BOOKS:
WWW.ONMETATRON.COM/SHOP

Fawn Parker is a writer from Toronto. She studies creative writing and English literature at Concordia University in Montreal. Her work has been published in Joyland, Hobart, and The Quietus. This is her first book.